Almost Twins

by Linda Jean Singleton

illustrated by Don Robison

Published by Worthington Press
10100 SBF Drive, Pinellas Park, Florida 34666

Copyright ©1991 by Worthington Press

Printed in the United States of America
10 9 8 7 6 5 4 3 2 1

ISBN 0-87406-452-X

For David—
my wonderful husband

One

SHE looked like me. She had the same long, strawberry-blond hair, the same sprinkle of freckles across her nose, and the same shade of sky blue eyes. We even had the same birthday, October 29th. We were exactly alike. She was my very best friend in the whole world. We shared the same smile—that is until I turned away from the mirror.

"Only in a mirror," I muttered angrily, flinging myself onto the hotel bed. "Why couldn't I have been born a twin?"

I rolled over and reached for my teddy bear, Sophie. Her sagging button eyes stared at me blankly. "It just isn't fair," I said to Sophie out loud. "April and Candy are so lucky to be twins.

They look alike, talk alike, and get all the attention. I'm always left out of everything. I'm just plain Frankie. Why couldn't I have been born a twin, too?"

I gave my pillow a punch. It was bad enough being the youngest in the family. But having older sisters who were identical twins was even worse.

Just then I heard the door open. I turned around and saw April's face peering at me. I knew it was April because she has a tiny mole at the bottom of her left ear. Most people don't notice it, but I do. It's the only way I can tell April and Candy apart.

"What do you want?" I asked her.

April tossed a strand of light brown hair over her shoulder and smiled. "Mom wants to know if you want to go with us to the Sandland Hotel. That's where we register for the Lookalike Contest."

I glared at her. I usually loved vacations, and Santa Cruz was one of the neatest places to visit. But this time I was not thrilled. The only reason our family was spending a week in this touristy California city was because my sisters were entering a stupid contest for twins and triplets. And no one had even asked me if I wanted to go.

"No, I'd rather stay here," I answered.

"All by yourself?" April asked. She looked at me strangely.

"Why not? Twelve is old enough to stay alone."

"I guess so," April said.

"Maybe I'll walk down to the boardwalk," I said. "All of the stores and rides are right on the beach."

"Well, you are planning to watch Candy and me compete in the Lookalike Contest, aren't you? There's a good chance we'll win."

"Yeah, I guess I'll be there," I said. "But if I had a twin, I'm sure I could beat you two."

"You're crazy! Candy and I are identical. Hardly anyone can tell us apart!"

I paused and smiled. "I can."

"Okay, do what you want to do today. I'll tell Mom that you don't want to come with us."

"Tell her that I'll be on the beach," I said.

"Have it your way. See you later," April said and walked out of the room.

I felt kind of weird after April left. It's not that I really wanted to be included in all the silly twin activities. It's just that I didn't feel that I fit in here somehow. After all, the whole point of this vacation was the Lookalike Contest. It was Dad's idea for Candy and April to enter. He thought it would do us all good to get away—especially Mom. She's an obstetrician, a doctor who delivers babies, and she has trouble turning away patients. It was good for her to relax once in a while.

But me—well, I just wasn't in the mood for a vacation. And all the activities here are twin-related. If only I had a twin, life would be great. *Oh, well*, I thought to myself, *a walk and some fresh air would do me good.*

I put on my swimsuit beneath my shorts and top in case I felt like going swimming in the ocean. I headed out the front door of the Santa Cruz Bed and Breakfast Inn where we were staying. Even if I didn't like this whole vacation, the inn was a pretty nice place. It was full of antiques and had all kinds of nooks and crannies. The front steps creaked as I ran down them toward the boardwalk.

The fresh salty sprays of the ocean and the cool breeze felt good. For the first time that day, I felt like I might enjoy this vacation after all. I followed a wooden stairway down to the beach and skipped happily along the surf. If I could just stay away from Candy and April, I would be fine.

The beach was swarming with people. I guess July is a really popular time to come here. I kept walking as I looked away for someone who looked like "friend" material. What I needed was a girl my own age to hang out with.

I flipped my hair over my shoulder and stopped to watch all the people. Everybody seemed older than I was—more April and Candy's age. At first, I was surprised to notice a lot of twins, but then I remembered we were here for the Lookalike Contest.

As I walked along, I even saw boy triplets, who looked like they could be in high school. They were playing Frisbee. As I walked past them, one of them yelled, "Hey, Joanna, catch!" Then he threw the Frisbee right at me.

I ducked and watched as the orange disk sailed over my head. It landed in the lap of a woman who was sitting beneath a large umbrella.

The boy who had called out to me gave me a dirty look as he ran to get his Frisbee. His identical brothers gave me angry looks, too, as though I had messed up their game on purpose.

I hurried down the beach, wondering if all the boys in Santa Cruz were so weird. I reached a quiet area that bordered a rocky cliff and waded into the ocean. The water felt cold to me at first, so I only went in up to my knees. After a few minutes, I got used to the temperature. I shut my eyes and dived in.

When I came back up to the surface, I paddled around for a while. Swimming is about my favorite thing to do. I loved taking swimming lessons—until I had to go off the diving board. Swimming is one thing, but jumping off a board into deep water is another. I got a yucky feeling in my stomach just thinking about it.

I splashed around some more. I practiced a weird stroke that I'd made up. It's kind of a cross between the backstroke and the crawl. It felt good to be on my own. Then, suddenly, I glanced up and saw someone swimming right toward me.

Darn, I thought. *I hope it isn't going to be another weird boy.*

As the swimmer came closer, I saw that it

wasn't a boy at all. It was a girl. I couldn't help but stare at her. Her face looked really familiar. It seemed like I knew her from somewhere.

Maybe this girl was someone from my school. Santa Cruz was a popular place to vacation after all. In my mind, I ran through everybody in my class, but I still couldn't figure it out.

The swimmer was only a few feet away when suddenly I knew. She wasn't anyone from my school at all. She wasn't anyone that I'd ever met before.

I gasped and just stared. It wasn't possible. But it was really happening. Those blue eyes, the turned up nose, and big grin were mine! It was like looking into a mirror. This girl was my double!

Two

"**W**OW!" the girl exclaimed when she got a good look at me. "I can't believe it."

"We look exactly the same," I said.

"Unless I'm dreaming," the other *me* said. "You must be a better swimmer than I am, because I'm pooped. Let's head for shore."

I nodded, nearly swallowing some water. "Let's go."

"I'm Joanna Trent," the girl said after we had plopped down on a large rock that was nestled in a little cove. We just kept staring at each other. It was unbelievable.

"I'm Frankie Stein," I said politely.

"Frankie? Isn't that a boy's name?"

It seemed like everyone asked me that question. "Well, my name is really Frances Anne Stein, but I like Frankie better. Ever since I wore a Frankenstein costume for Halloween when I was five years old, everyone has called me Frankie."

"Oh," Joanna said and nodded. "Your hair is a lot longer than mine is," she observed.

"And yours isn't as red as mine," I said. "But other than that..." my voice trailed off as I slowly shook my head and stared at Joanna.

"Yeah. Isn't this great? We're doubles. Think of the possibilities," Joanna said, her blue eyes full of excitement.

"Possibilities?" I echoed. "Like what?"

"Oh, I'm sure we'll be able to pull a few pranks. And I even know some people we can pull them on."

Joanna was getting way ahead of me. I wasn't thinking about what we could do as twins—I was so stunned just looking at her! "Hey! Are you from around here?" I asked her.

"No, I'm from Sacramento. And you?"

"I'm from Davis," I told her. "I think it's only about half an hour from Sacramento. So, how old are you? I'm 12," I said.

"I turned 12 last month. What grade are you in?" Joanna asked excitedly.

"I'll be in seventh. My parents said I started kindergarten late because my birthday is late in the fall," I explained.

"We're in the same grade then. That's great. I've always wanted a twin. You can't imagine what it's like having triplet brothers."

"Triplet brothers! So, that's why those boys threw a Frisbee at me and called me Joanna. They thought I was you!" I recalled, laughing. "I've always wanted a twin, too. My twin sisters are 16. And all they think about is boys."

Joanna looked at me in amazement. "You have twin sisters, and I have triplet brothers. What a riot!"

"If you have triplet brothers, you must be here for the Lookalike Contest, too," I said.

"Yeah. My brothers think they're going to win," Joanna said and rolled her eyes.

I smiled. "Yeah, my sisters think they will, too. They're pretty confident about winning the contest."

"What kinds of things do you like to do?" Joanna asked me.

"I collect stuffed animals. I love to swim. And sometimes I write poems," I said.

"Poems? That's neat! Maybe you can write one for me one day. I like math better than English," she said.

"You like math?" I asked with surprise. "How could anyone like math? Do you play any sports?"

"Lots of them," Joanna said. "I play basketball and softball. But I especially love gymnastics. I can do a somersault on the balance beam and four back flips in a row."

"Swimming is my favorite sport," I told her.

"I guess we really don't have that much in common," Joanna said.

I smiled. "Sure we do. We're in the same grade, and we look like twins."

"Not exactly like twins," Joanna said slowly.

"What do you mean?" I asked.

"Well, your hair is longer than mine is, and yours is reddish blond," she pointed out.

I nodded. "My sisters always say that I have the best hair in the family. I've never really had it cut a lot before. It's just been trimmed once in a while."

"It *is* really pretty," Joanna complimented. "But it's kind of in the way."

I felt my stomach do a flip-flop.

"What do you mean?" I asked slowly. I wasn't so sure I wanted to hear Joanna's idea.

"Well, you have twin sisters, and I have triplet brothers. We've always been left out of everything, right? But now that we have found a twin, why not make the most of it?"

"I don't know. If it means cutting my hair..." I nearly choked on the words. "I don't think so," I said finally.

"But it's the only way," Joanna said. "And just think of all the neat stuff we can do if we look alike!"

"But my hair! I can't do it!"

"Well, I can't grow mine as long as yours. But I would be willing to change the color. Brown hair is kind of dull, and I've always wanted to have reddish hair anyway," she added with a giggle.

I hesitated. What would I look like if I cut my hair? I just couldn't do it. But if I didn't, I'd never know what it was like to be a twin. And that was something I'd always dreamed about.

It was a painful decision, but I decided to go ahead with it finally. "All right," I moaned. "All right. I'll do it."

"Great!" Joanna shouted, startling a group of children who had started to make a sand castle near us. "Once our hair looks the same, no one will be able to tell us apart. It'll be so much fun! Just wait."

*   *   *   *   *

"You haven't changed your mind?" Joanna asked as we entered a hair salon a few minutes later.

"No, I said I would do it. I just wish there was some other way to make my hair look like yours," I mumbled. I climbed onto the swivel salon chair and nervously pulled at the corners of the plastic smock that the hairstylist draped over me.

"Are you comfortable?" the stylist asked as she spun the chair around so I was facing her. "Have you decided how you would like your hair styled?"

I nodded and pointed at Joanna. "Yes, I want my hair to be just like hers."

The stylist looked curiously at Joanna and then back at me. Her smile widened and she raised one eyebrow. "Twins? Oh, you two must be here for the Lookalike Contest."

"Yes, we are," Joanna said quickly.

"Okay, then," the hairstylist said. "This will be a great haircut for the summer."

I fidgeted in my chair. My stomach began doing flip-flops. I watched Joanna sit down in a chair and reach for a magazine to read. *This is it*, I thought sadly. *Good-bye, long hair.*

I couldn't bear to watch, so I closed my eyes. I felt the wetness of water being sprayed onto my hair, and then I felt the combing and snipping. It felt like 20 long minutes of pure torture.

And then it was over.

"I'm all finished," the hairstylist said. "You can open your eyes now."

I opened one eye and then the other. My hair didn't look so bad. I looked more grown-up with shorter hair. And, except for the color of my hair, I looked exactly like Joanna.

"My goodness, you look just like your sister now!" the stylist exclaimed as she untied the smock. "If your hair was brown instead of strawberry blond, I certainly wouldn't be able to tell you two apart."

I brushed off some wisps of hair that were sticking to my T-shirt. "That's what we're hoping for," I said. "We're both going to be redheads. Right, Joanna?"

Joanna nodded. "Yes, I'll keep my part of the deal."

I paid the eight dollars for my haircut and gave the hairstylist a tip. I was using a lot of the allowance money I'd managed to save up. But having a twin of my own was worth the money to me.

As we walked outside, I turned to Joanna. "So, how do we dye your hair?" I asked.

"We have to buy a package of hair color. I've seen my mom buy it at the drugstore."

"Your mom dyes her hair?" I asked in surprise. I couldn't imagine my mom doing that.

"Sure. Lots of women do. My mom does it to keep the gray out of her hair. She says that she has...uh, what does she call it? Oh, yeah, premature gray hair."

"Oh," I said. It sounded terrible to me.

"And I've seen her do it lots of times. It looks really easy. It's just like shampooing your hair. You should have no problem doing my hair."

"Me?" I asked in panic. "You want *me* to do it? Why me?"

Joanna just shrugged. "Of course, I want you to do it. I can't do it by myself, and it costs a lot of money to have it done at a salon."

"But I've never seen anyone dye hair before. What if I mess up? Your hair might end up with huge red or purple spots. Or, what if all of your hair falls out?"

Joanna gave me a disgusted look. "Hey, you're not chickening out on me, are you?" she asked with a teasing grin.

"No, I'm not."

"Good. Because this is our big chance to find out what being twins is all about. Right?" Joanna asked.

"You're right. I just don't want to do anything that will ruin your hair. But if you're not scared about doing it, then neither am I," I said with a big grin. I knew being twins meant as much to Joanna as it did to me. I just hoped that she couldn't tell that my stomach was in knots.

Three

WE walked over to the drugstore at the far end of the boardwalk. We quickly scanned the aisles until we found the section with all of the hair dyes. I couldn't believe my eyes. It seemed like hair coloring came in every shade in the world.

Joanna held one box at a time near my hair until she found a color that seemed to be a close match. We paid for the dye and then hurried back to her hotel room to get started.

"Oh, look, Frankie! We even get plastic gloves with this brand," Joanna said as she opened the box on the bathroom counter. She held up a see-through pair of gloves. "Aren't these neat?"

"What are they for?" I asked. Joanna un-folded a piece of paper that had all the direc-tions written out. "I guess they're for you to wear while you're shampooing the dye into my hair."

I took the gloves and slipped them on. They were kind of big on me, but at least they would keep my hands from turning funny colors.

"What do we do first?" I asked.

Joanna read each step aloud, and in less than an hour, it was over. Joanna's hair came out a soft shade of strawberry blond. It looked exactly like mine!

We stood in front of the mirror in Joanna's hotel room and admired ourselves. I had to admit our new hairstyles looked great.

"We did it! We really look like twins!" I said.

"Well, *we* think we look like twins. But we need to try it out and see if we can fool other people," Joanna suggested eagerly.

"How are we going to do that?" I asked.

"Well," Joanna began, "we could go down

near the beach shops and see if anyone says anything to us. Or, we could find your sisters or my brothers and see what they say. I wonder if they'll be able to tell the difference."

"Shouldn't we dress alike?" I asked. The thought of trying to fool her triplet brothers definitely made me nervous. I'm not a good liar to begin with, and lying to boys would be especially hard.

"Yeah, you're right. We should try to dress the same. We can buy matching T-shirts at a shop along the boardwalk. But for fun right now, let's just wear a couple of my T-shirts. I have two that look about the same." Joanna dug into her suitcase and pulled out two shirts. "Here," she said, "put this one on."

I changed quickly, and we were ready for the big test. I was excited about exploring the boardwalk. I had scanned it from the beach, but I was looking forward to the arcades and shopping. It looked colorful and full of fun. There was even an amusement park that ran all along the beach.

The roller coasters looked exciting, but there was no way I'd ever go on one. I could handle merry-go-rounds and the old-time car rides, but nothing that was bouncy. My stomach did too many flip-flops.

The boardwalk was really crowded and noisy, just like the beach had been earlier. The noise from the rides, the games, and the crowds of people was incredible.

Joanna pulled me into the first T-shirt shop she saw. We picked out matching pink T-shirts and quickly paid for them. *There goes the rest of my allowance,* I thought.

"Come on, Frankie," Joanna said as we left the store. She pulled me toward the rides. "Let's go on the Jet Star. It looks great."

My stomach started doing flip-flops again, and I stopped walking. "That's a roller coaster, isn't it?" Joanna nodded, and I shook my head. "No, I can't go on that. Rides like that make me sick."

"You don't like roller coasters?" Joanna asked in amazement.

"I threw up on one when I was in third grade. Everyone was really mad at me, so I've stuck to easier rides ever since," I explained.

"Easy rides are not my idea of fun," Joanna complained. "Oh, well, everybody has fears of some kind, I guess." She smiled finally.

I smiled back. I looked up to see three dark-headed boys climbing the stairway from the beach to the boardwalk.

"Hey, are those your brothers?" I asked. "I think they're the guys who yelled at me to catch the Frisbee earlier."

"Where? Oh, yeah, they're my brothers," Joanna said.

"Oh, no! They're coming this way," I warned her. My stomach felt sick again.

"This is perfect," Joanna said excitedly. "Now we'll find out if we really look alike."

"How?" I asked her.

"Go over to my brothers and pretend to be

me," she said encouragingly.

"No way!" I protested. "They'll know for sure I'm not you. Besides, I don't even know their names."

"Brandon, Bobby, and Steve," Joanna rattled off. "But don't worry about that. I just call them all Trip for short so I don't have to worry about getting their names wrong."

"Trip?" I echoed.

"Yeah. It's short for triplet," Joanna said with a grin. "The Trips used to be a lot of fun. They used to let me be a part of their games and stuff. But when they turned 16, every-thing started changing. Now all they care about is girls. Their brains have turned to mush. They'll be easy to fool."

I leaned against the railing to consider Joanna's idea. My eyes drifted down to where Joanna's brothers were buying ride tickets. The boys looked like they were having fun. And Joanna was their sister, so they couldn't be too hard to get along with...could they?

I was nervous. I turned back to Joanna. "What should I say to them?"

"Just say anything that pops into your head," she coaxed. "You can ask them about the Lookalike Contest." Joanna pointed and urged, "Hey, we better hurry. They've finished buying their tickets. We can't lose them now."

I handed Joanna my new T-shirt to hold for me. Then I took a deep breath and started down the steps toward Joanna's brothers. Joanna hid behind a large pillar to listen as I talked with them.

"Hey, Trips," I called, lowering my voice so I sounded more like Joanna.

The boys stopped walking and turned in my direction. "Yeah. What do you want?" one of them asked. He wore a blue T-shirt with a surfing design on the front.

"Nothing," I mumbled. "I just wondered how things went with registration. Are you signed up for the Lookalike Contest?"

"Sure. But registration was hours ago,"

another of the Trips said. This guy was wearing a green shirt and a pair of mirrored sunglasses. He pulled off his sunglasses and stared at me. "What happened to your hair?"

I hadn't thought about that. "Uh, I wanted a change. I thought it'd be fun to be a redhead for a while," I explained as casually as I could.

"Why would you want to do that?" asked the third Trip. "What's wrong with brown hair like we have?"

"I just want my own look. So, where's Mom?" I asked, trying to get him off the subject of my hair.

"Oh, she's talking with all of the convention people," the same Trip explained. "We were lucky to get out of there before Mom began introducing us to everyone." I decided that this Trip would be the easiest to remember since his hair was the curliest of the three.

Suddenly, I realized that I had fooled them. They really did think that I was Joanna.

"Yeah, we were lucky," the Trip wearing the

blue T-shirt added with a grin. "There's no way I want to be stuck inside all day when there's so much going on outside."

"Yeah!" the curly-haired Trip said with a chuckle. "There are girls our age everywhere around here."

"We met these really nice twins just a few minutes ago. They had pretty, brown hair and cute smiles. I think they said they're names were Candy and April," the Trip wearing the green shirt said.

"Candy and April!" I exclaimed, almost forgetting who I was supposed to be.

"Do you know them or something?" the same Trip asked.

"No, not really," I lied. *It was just like my sisters to zero in on these cute guys,* I thought.

"Hey, I want to go on the rides," Curly-hair said. "We need a fourth person to ride the Jet Star with us. Let's go, Jo."

"Yeah, come on, Jo," Blue-shirt added.

"NO!" I screamed. I knew I was acting like

Frankie and not Joanna, but I couldn't help it. "I don't want to go on the rides. I feel sick."

"Are you serious? The Jet Star has always been your favorite. I can't believe you don't want to go. There's something weird going on. If I didn't know better, Jo, I'd say you weren't our sister," said Blue-shirt.

"W-what do you mean?" I stammered. "Of course, I'm your sister." My stomach felt queasy, and my knees were wobbly.

"Then come on," Blue-shirt said.

I was being stared at by six blue eyes, all waiting for me to get in line for the ride with them. I took a deep breath and stepped in line for the Jet Star. The line moved too quickly for me, because in just a few minutes I was seated beside Blue-shirt, and the roller coaster car was crawling steadily up the first hill.

My heart was pounding in my ears, and my hands felt cold and numb. I had tucked my feet into the corners of the car and wrapped my fingers in a tight grip around the bar in front of me. The kids in front of us had raised their arms into the air like they weren't even going to hold on at all. They were crazy to try that.

"You look funny, Jo," Blue-shirt said. "You're not really sick, are you?"

"Uh, not yet," I mumbled. As we reached the top of the hill, I gripped the safety handles with a life-or-death squeeze. There was no turning back now. With a jolt, the Jet Star sprang into life and leaped down the first hill.

"Here we go!" Blue-shirt yelled above the roar of screams. I closed my eyes and prayed for the ride to be over. I felt myself going up...up...up...and then DOWN! My eyes flew open, and I realized I was screaming at the top of my lungs. But no one paid any attention to me. Suddenly, I didn't feel so sick. And somewhere in the middle of the ride I realized that I was having fun!

When the ride finally stopped, Joanna's brothers jumped out of their seats. My knees were a little wobbly, but I followed them as if I had done this every day of my life.

"Boy, that was great!" Curly-hair said.

"It was wild!" Blue-shirt agreed. "It was so wild that Joanna's screams ruined my hearing for good."

Green-shirt laughed and looked at me. "Hey, want to go on the Jet Star again, Jo?"

I shook my head. "Not now. I think I'll go get something to eat."

"I know where you should go," Curly-hair said. "There's a great stand at the end of the boardwalk that has extra large onion rings."

"Ugh!" I made a face. I hated onions more than just about anything.

Joanna's brothers were looking at me strangely. "But you love onion rings," one of them said. "Jo, you're acting really weird today."

I better get out of this mess—and fast, I decided. I mumbled something about having lots of things to do. I walked away and tried not to think about the strange looks I knew they were giving me. I headed for Joanna's hiding place behind the pillar.

Joanna was laughing so hard that she could barely talk.

"How did you like the Jet Star?" she asked me in between giggles.

"I could kill you for that! I'm just lucky that I didn't get sick. You know, I'm still trembling."

"I'm sorry, Frankie. But you really did look funny," Joanna said.

"It's not funny to be scared to death," I argued.

"I said that I'm sorry. Was the Jet Star really that bad? I think it's terrific," Joanna said.

I shrugged. "Oh, it was okay after all," I said. "But I could use something to drink."

"And I'm hungry." Joanna handed me my shopping bag. "How about splitting some onion rings with me?"

"Not onion rings again," I said. "You sound just like your brothers."

"What's wrong with onion rings?" Joanna asked.

"I hate them. I hate anything with onions just about as much as I love chocolate."

"You love chocolate?" Joanna asked. "Yuck. I don't like sweet stuff."

"And I hate onion rings."

We looked at each other and giggled.

"So, how do you feel about corn dogs?" I asked.

"I like them," Joanna admitted.

"Good. Let's go get some."

"Yeah. We have something to celebrate," she announced.

"Celebrate?" I asked her.

"Yeah. Our twin test worked. We're really twins now. My mush-head brothers didn't even know it wasn't me."

"You're right," I agreed. "It really worked. I was even beginning to have fun until they brought up the Jet Star and onion rings."

"Hey, you know what we can do next?"

Joanna's eyes sparkled at the thought of her new plan.

"What?" I asked. "I think we've done enough already."

"No, not yet. Why fool just my brothers when we can have so much more fun? We're going to enter the Lookalike Contest—and we're going to win!"

Four

BY the time I got back to the Bed and Breakfast Inn later that evening, I was full and tired. Joanna and I had eaten lots of junk food while we were shopping along the boardwalk. The idea of crawling underneath my covers and going to sleep sounded great. But first I wanted to say hello to my mom

"Hi, Mom," I called out as I walked into the room.

Mom raised a finger to her lips and pointed to the phone receiver that she held up to her ear. "Shhh," she whispered. "I'll be off in a couple of minutes. I'm talking to Mrs. Welch."

"I can't believe she called *here*," I said. Mrs.

Welch was one of Mom's patients who was going to have a baby.

"Frankie, I'm busy right now," Mom said in a tired voice. "Could we talk later?" she asked, looking at my hair with a puzzled look.

"Sure, Mom," I said.

Mom flashed me a smile and then started talking to Mrs. Welch again.

I looked around the room for someone to talk to. Both bedrooms were empty. I wondered where Dad and the twins were.

I heard some noise out in the hallway, and then the entry door flew open. Dad, Candy, and April were laughing at something as they walked into the room.

Mom gave us all a look that said we'd better be quiet.

Dad glanced over to me. "Is it a patient?"

I nodded and sat down in the padded vinyl chair near the window.

Suddenly, Candy's eyes opened wide in surprise. "Frankie! Your hair!" she cried.

"What happened to you?" April shrieked.

"I had my hair cut," I said. "Do you like it?

"Why would you have your hair cut, Frankie? Your hair was so beautiful the way it was," Candy said.

"Then I guess it still is. It's just a little shorter," I said.

"A little shorter?" April asked. "It's more than a little shorter."

Dad gave me one of his thoughtful looks. "Frances Anne, what is this all about? Why did you go out and have your hair cut?"

I lifted my chin. "I just decided to, Dad. It's no big deal."

"Did your mother go with you?" he asked.

"No, she didn't," I admitted.

Dad frowned. "You mean you had your hair cut without getting permission?"

"I didn't think I had to," I explained. "I mean, it's my hair. I should be able to get it cut if I feel like it."

"Maybe," Dad said slowly, "but I'd feel a lot

better about this if you had discussed it with your mom or me first."

"Why? Because I'm not one of the twins?" I asked. I knew I shouldn't have said that, but I couldn't help it. Sometimes, it seemed like the twins had all the privileges. If Candy or April wanted to do something, they didn't have to ask permission.

"Frances, just tell me why you wanted to have shorter hair," Dad said. He stared at me and waited for my answer.

I wanted to tell Dad about meeting Joanna, but I decided it wasn't right to share our secret. Besides, my family would never go along with our plan to enter the Lookalike Contest. I wondered if Joanna's family was giving her a hassle, too.

"I just wanted a cooler haircut," I said. "And I wanted a new style. Don't be upset, Dad."

"I guess you haven't really done anything wrong," Dad decided. "I'm sorry for jumping to conclusions, Frances. It's just such a big change. But you do look very nice. You look more grown-up."

"Oh, she doesn't look that grown-up, Dad," Candy said. Candy always thought she knew everything. I ignored her and asked my father about their day.

"Everything went fine," Dad said with a grin. "Your sisters registered for the contest. They should do well. I saw dozens of twins today, but none of them compared with your sisters."

Candy tugged on April's arm. "Let's go pick out what we're going to wear for the dinner tomorrow night."

"Let's wear our blue dresses," April suggested.

"No, my blue one has a rip in the sleeve. How about our pink dresses?" Candy asked.

"Maybe," April replied.

I watched my sisters walk into their room and close the door. Their room was my room, too, but I was never invited to join in their discussions. I didn't feel like starting an argument, so I decided to wait a while before going in to change into my nightgown. Sometimes I felt like I didn't have any rights as a member of this family.

Maybe I didn't. I wasn't one of the Princess Twins.

* * * * *

"I don't know how we're going to do this. How can we register as twins if we aren't even sisters?" I asked Joanna early the next morning.

Joanna just smiled back at me, and once again I had the strange sensation of looking into a mirror. We were wearing our new matching pink T-shirts. We had left our hotel rooms before our families were even awake. It was time to get the big plan underway.

"Just follow me," Joanna said as she led her way through the Sandland Hotel. "I heard my brothers talk about registration. It was a breeze. We just tell them our names, ages, and other simple stuff. And that's it."

"Really?" I asked. Joanna seemed to have all the answers, but this whole contest thing still made me nervous.

"Sure. It'll be easy," Joanna assured me. "We just have to go up to the Lookalike Contest registration desk on the next floor."

"Okay," I said reluctantly. "Let's get this over with."

We headed toward the escalator. Suddenly, I was really scared of getting caught.

"Hey, Joanna. What did you tell your parents about your hair?" I asked, hoping she had come up with a good answer.

"Oh, I said that I'd always thought it was neat how Mom always created new looks with hair color, and that I wanted to try it, too. She wasn't thrilled at first, but at least she didn't get mad about it," Joanna said with a grin.

"What about your dad?" I asked.

"He just stared at my hair for a while. Then he admitted that he liked it," Joanna said.

We stepped off of the escalator, and soon we were standing in front of a hand-painted sign that said "Lookalike Contest Registration."

A skinny man with a round bald spot looked up as we walked toward the desk. He wore a name tag that said "T.M. Burns."

"Hello, girls. What can I do for you?" he asked.

"We want to sign up for the Lookalike Contest."

Mr. Burns smiled and sorted through a pile of papers on his desk. He pulled out a sheet of white paper and a pen. "All right. What are your names?"

"I'm Jo—I mean," Joanna stopped and then said quickly, "I'm Anna Trent."

"And I'm Fran—"

Joanna cut in, "Francesca Trent. She's my sister."

"Yeah," I added, thankful that Joanna had stopped me from blurting out my real name. It would have looked weird for twin sisters to have different last names.

Mr. Burns went on, "And what's your address?"

I let Joanna answer, "4840 Perina Way, Sacramento, California."

"And when is your birthday?"

Joanna said "June" at the same time I said "October."

"Well, which is it?" Mr. Burns asked, looking puzzled. "June or October. I don't believe it's possible to have twins born four months apart."

"We were born on October 29th," I said quickly.

Mr. Burns gave us a weird look, but he continued to jot down information on his form. After a few minutes, he said, "Well, that's it. You're registered...that is, once I have your parents' permission."

My mouth dropped open, and my eyes opened widened. So did Joanna's.

"W-What?" I asked.

"You can be part of the preliminary judging this afternoon. Just have either your mother or your father stop by to give their okay before 2:00."

"Before 2:00?" Joanna echoed, gnawing nervously on one of her fingernails.

"Yes. The Lookalike Contest is being held in two parts. The first judging will be in a few hours. And if you're one of the five sets of lookalikes chosen in the girl category, you'll have the chance to compete again tomorrow on the beach bandstand."

"But our parents are busy today. I don't know if I can find them in time," I said.

"Yeah. We might not be able to find them," Joanna agreed. "Can't you register us anyway? Besides, you already spoke to our mom. She was here yesterday when she signed up our triplet brothers."

"She was?" Mr. Burns looked surprised. "Oh, yes, I remember your brothers."

Joanna nodded. "Since she's already given her permission for my brothers, isn't that good enough for us, too?"

Mr. Burns shook his head in confusion. "I don't understand. Why didn't your mother register you two when she registered your brothers?"

Joanna and I looked helplessly at each other.

"Hey," Joanna finally said, "that's a good question. I wonder why Mom didn't register us, too. Did she tell you why, Francesca?"

"No, she didn't, Anna," I mumbled, hoping we could get out of this soon.

From down the hall, we could hear the elevator door opening. Suddenly, Mr. Burns smiled widely. He pointed to the elevator and said, "Well, this must be your lucky day, girls. Isn't that your mother now?"

Joanna jerked around to see. "Oh, no!" she

whispered with her back to Mr. Burns. "It *is* my mom, and she's coming this way." She grabbed my arm and pulled me a few feet away from the registration area.

"Your mother! But she can't see us together," I whispered back. I had to escape fast! I quickly slid around the corner and into the rest room. After my heart stopped pounding, I peeked out the door to see what was happening.

I could hear Joanna talking to her mom. "I thought you were going to hang around with your brothers today," Mrs. Trent said.

"I was, but they wanted to meet some other kids," Joanna said.

"I asked your father to have breakfast with me here at the hotel, but I can't find him. Have you seen him? I've been looking everywhere for him," Mrs. Trent explained.

"I haven't seen him. Have you called the room?" Joanna asked her mom.

"Yes, and he wasn't there," Mrs. Trent

replied. "By the way, what are you doing here?"

Joanna's face reddened. "Uh, I'm just finding out about the Lookalike Contest."

"Why didn't you ask me about it? I took care of all the details yesterday."

Mr. Burns interrupted, "Not all the details, Mrs. Trent. I still need to get your official permission."

I held my breath. *Oh, no,* I thought, *our plan is going to be ruined.*

"My permission?" Mrs. Trent echoed. "But I gave my permission yesterday. Don't you remember?" She waved her hand impatiently and then added, "I really don't have time for this again. Yes, I give my permission. Now, I have to find my husband. See you later, dear," she said to Joanna and started to walk away.

Joanna jumped up happily. She took her mother by the arm. "I'll help you find Dad. Maybe he's waiting for you in the restaurant."

"Now that's an idea," Mrs. Trent replied as they walked away.

I let out the big breath I'd been holding in. I sneaked out of the rest room and peeked around the corner. I watched Joanna and her mother disappear down the hallway and into the elevator. I couldn't resist smiling to myself. We were registered. Joanna and I were officially twins!

Five

JOANNA and I were excited to spend another day hanging around the boardwalk. Mrs. Trent had been so relieved to track down her husband in the restaurant that she had given Joanna the okay to go to the boardwalk. Joanna had walked up behind me in a clothing boutique near our inn and had practically scared me to death.

"I can't believe we're registered. It was amazing how your mother helped us out even though she didn't know she was doing it," I said to Joanna as we walked out of the Sandland Hotel.

Joanna laughed. "Mom was great! We were pretty lucky."

I nodded. "Yeah. You know, we should have decided on whose birthday to use before we registered. I think Mr. Burns thought we were crazy. And after my mad dash for the bathroom, Mr. Burns must think we're the weirdest twins he's ever seen!"

"He's right! We are," Joanna teased.

I laughed. "Yeah, I guess most twins know more about each other than we do. And it takes a while to get used to people staring at us."

"I think that's the best part," Joanna said with a grin.

I smiled. Joanna sure seemed to love being the center of attention.

As we walked along the boardwalk, Joanna pointed to an outfit in the window of one of the shops.

"Hey, let's look in there. We're going to need some matching clothes for the banquet tonight, and for tomorrow if we're lucky enough to be picked today," she said.

Joanna didn't seem to mind spending all

her money. I hated spending all the baby-sitting money I'd been saving for a new bi-cycle. But I knew this would be much more fun. *Wouldn't it?*

I was excited about being a twin and being able to fool people. I was so tired of being in the shadow of the Princess Twins. It seemed like April and Candy received at least one matching outfit on every holiday and birth-day. Then they always went around trying to trick everyone. I got so sick of it.

But now it was my turn.

Joanna and I picked out T-shirts and tiny matching earrings. But most exciting was Joanna's idea for slogans to put across the front of our blue T-shirts. The slogans only made sense when we were standing side by side. One shirt said "She's Me," and the other said "I'm Her."

I hoped we would make it to the finals. I was dying to see the looks on Candy and April's faces when they saw that it was Joanna and

I on stage competing with them.

Before I knew it, it was 2:00, and Joanna and I had to rush to make our meeting with the judging committee. The committee turned out to be Mr. Burns and gray-haired twin sisters named Helen and Louise Dobbs.

"Anna and Francesca Trent," Mr. Burns read off of a sheet of paper. "This should be interesting." He adjusted his glasses and looked closely at us. "Which one is which?"

"I'm Anna," Joanna said.

"And I'm Francesca," I replied.

"Tell us about yourself, Anna," Helen Dobbs said, adjusting the hat that sat awkwardly on her head.

"Well, I'm in seventh grade. My favorite color is red. I'm vice president of my class, and I love gymnastics."

I was surprised. Joanna hadn't said anything to me about being on student council. Maybe we should have talked more before we went ahead and became instant twins.

"And you, Francesca?" Mr. Burns asked, breaking into my thoughts. "What things do you like?"

I fidgeted. "Uh, I like swimming. The butterfly is my best stroke. My favorite subject is English, and I read pretty fast. And my favorite color is lavender."

Louise smiled. "That's fine. Now tell us what being a twin means to you."

I froze. Just when I thought we were sailing along okay, they asked a tough question. How would I know what being a twin meant?

Joanna answered. "It means having a built-in friend. Francesca and I do almost everything together."

We do? I thought in panic, wishing I could look as relaxed as Joanna did. I wasn't very good at lying.

"It's fun wearing the same clothes, like these pink shirts we have on now. We bought them yesterday," I added truthfully. If I could rearrange the truth a little, it was okay. But

I couldn't just lie.

"Well you two certainly seem to get along well. You know that not all sisters, twins or not, are friends. Do you each have other friends, too?" Helen asked.

"I do stuff with the other kids on my gymnastics team," Joanna said. "We all go out for pizza sometimes."

"And what about you, Francesca? Tell us about your friends," Louise said.

"There's Jennifer Ming, who is in my English class. I have fun at her house. Her mom is really neat. One time, she made us caramel popcorn balls and rented some videos for us," I said. "Being friends with Jennifer is fun, but not as much fun as being a twin."

"What about your family? Do you have any other sisters or brothers?" Louise asked.

"I have two sis—" I began without thinking.

Joanna butted in to stop my confession.

"We have three brothers," she said loudly.

"Brothers?" murmured Helen. "We interviewed three Trent boys earlier. Could they be your brothers?"

Joanna nodded.

"That's unbelievable," Helen said. "They didn't even mention that they had twin sisters."

"Francesca," Louise continued, "how do you feel about your brothers? You must have quite an interesting family."

I thought of my sisters. I pictured them in my head as I answered her. "They're interesting...and confusing. They love to fool people, but I can always tell them apart. They like different things, but they look alike when they want to."

"Do you get along as well with your brothers as you do with your sister?" Mr. Burns asked.

Mr. Burns seemed to be staring at me, like he could tell I was hiding something from him.

I started fidgeting, and I could feel my cheeks turning pink. I spoke slowly, "No, not really. They're older and too busy for me...I mean, for us."

"Yeah," Joanna jumped in. "Our brothers can be real mush-brains. All they think about is girls! They don't seem to think we count much. And if Francesca and I aren't girls, then what are we?"

The judges laughed.

Louise looked pleased. "You two are definitely girls, and I'm amazed at how different you are. You have special interests and friends of your own. I get the feeling that you really are different people when I see you. You're not like so many twins where one starts a sentence and—"

"—the other finishes," Helen said with a giggle. "I agree that you two certainly are refreshing."

"Does that mean we pass?" Joanna asked eagerly.

"It wouldn't be fair for us to let you know right now," Mr. Burns said. "You'll have to wait until tonight at the banquet where the results will be posted. We still have more twins to interview."

"But did we do okay?" Joanna asked.

Helen and Louise smiled at us in a motherly way. Helen winked. "Don't worry, girls."

I let out a big sigh. They'd liked us!

*   *   *   *   *

During the short drive to the Lookalike Contest banquet that night, my mind was buzzing. I looked over at my sisters who sat beside me. They were busy fixing each other's hair so that they looked exactly alike. Joanna and I had to get through the evening somehow without anybody discovering our secret. We had to fool our families, and that wasn't going to be easy. I could hide things from Mom and Dad pretty easily, but keeping a secret from my snoopy sisters was just about im-possible.

Dad pulled our car into the hotel parking lot. I had to see Joanna for a few minutes. We had some things to decide for the next day if we were picked for the contest. Somehow I had to get away from my family before we all were settled at our table.

I quickly turned to my mom. "Can I go meet up with a girl I met today?" I asked.

"By yourself?" Mom asked as she shut the car door.

I nodded. "Sure. I know where she'll be. And I'll be okay."

Mom turned to Dad. "What do you think? Do you think she'll be all right walking around this place alone?"

"If Frankie is old enough to baby-sit, I guess she's old enough to meet a friend on her own for a little while," Dad decided. "Just be sure to stay close to the banquet area, Frankie. And I want you to be back at our table by the time dinner is served. Okay?"

I gave them each a quick hug. "Thanks. I'll be back soon. Bye."

Then I hurried off toward the hotel entrance.

I hurried inside to meet Joanna near the same rest room I had hidden in earlier that afternoon.

I smiled as I rounded the corner and saw my "twin" wearing the same shirt that I had on.

Joanna's face was full of excitement. "Hey, you look great!" she said. "Let's go find out where today's results are posted."

"Good idea. I'm just dying to know if we made it," I said.

The large banquet room was crowded. There were kids of all ages running around everywhere.

"Hey, there's a bulletin board," Joanna said and pointed over to the far corner of the room. "Let's go see if that's where the results are."

A pit seemed to grow inside my stomach as I followed Joanna through the aisle of tables. I was suddenly nervous. I wasn't sure if I was nervous because I was scared that we wouldn't make the list or because I was terrified that we would.

"Look, Frankie!" Joanna yelled, pointing to the white paper that was tacked up to the bulletin board. "We made it. I just knew we would. Oh, Frankie, we did it."

"We did?" I asked in amazement. This was what I had wanted, so why were my knees knocking together?

"Oh, no," Joanna said suddenly. "My brothers didn't make it. They can be big pains sometimes, but I was hoping that they'd make the finals."

"What about my sisters?" I asked quickly.

Joanna pointed to the top of the list. "Yeah, they made it. So they'll be competing against us."

I was glad that my sisters had made it, but

I was getting more nervous all the time. What would Candy and April do when saw us walk up on stage for the finals?

"One of us should get away from here," I said sud⎯⎯ly. "From now on, we'll have to be extra ca⎯⎯⎯⎯⎯⎯⎯⎯⎯⎯⎯ters don't see us togethe⎯⎯⎯⎯⎯⎯⎯⎯⎯⎯ find out our secret a⎯⎯⎯⎯⎯⎯⎯⎯⎯ve aren't really twins."

"You⎯⎯⎯⎯⎯⎯⎯⎯⎯ us?" Joanna asked ⎯⎯⎯⎯⎯⎯⎯

"Of ⎯⎯⎯⎯⎯⎯⎯⎯⎯⎯⎯don't know my sisters, Joanna. They do⎯⎯⎯⎯ me. They think I'm just a brat." I sighed. "If they do find out our plan," I said softly, "we're finished for sure."

Six

JOANNA took off to see what her family was doing. But my feet seemed glued to the floor. I couldn't seem to take my eyes off of the results that were loosely tacked to the bulletin board.

Suddenly, I felt a tap on my shoulder.

I expected to turn around and see Joanna. I thought that maybe she'd forgotten to tell me something. But it wasn't her. It was one of Joanna's brothers, but I had no idea which one it was. For a second, I stood there tongue-tied.

"How did you get here?" he asked. He had a strange puzzled look on his face. "I just left the table a second ago, and you had just sat down to talk with Mom and Dad."

I tried to think of a clever answer, but nothing popped into my head. "It's too much fun being here to stay at the table for very long," I said quickly. "And I wanted to see the contest results."

He frowned at the bulletin board. "Then I guess you saw that we didn't make the finals. Brandon and Steve are really bummed about it."

"Aren't you upset, too?" I asked him. I relaxed a little. I was glad to know that it was Bobby I was talking to.

He shook his head and grinned a little. "No, I really don't care about the competition. Actually, I'm happy that we don't have to do all that stuff anymore. I didn't want to get up on that bandstand tomorrow. It's so embarrassing to have everybody staring at you."

"You really feel that way?" I asked. I couldn't believe that he was happy about losing the contest. My sisters would have been furious.

"The whole contest thing was Mom's idea anyway. I just went along because Brandon and Steve thought it was fun to get all the attention." Bobby grinned. "But there are lots of cute girls in the contest. That makes the trip here worthwhile."

I grinned, too. "Have you seen the twins you talked about yesterday?"

Bobby's grin widened. "Yeah. I really like April. I think she's sweet. And Brandon thinks Candy is neat. And all Steve cares about is Lauren at home."

"So, you like April?" I echoed. I was curious about why he liked my sister. I knew she was cute, but I couldn't imagine why someone would think she was sweet.

"Yeah, a lot," he said. "She seems really down to earth and nice. There's nothing snotty about her. Candy's okay, too, but she's more Brandon's type. Hey, I haven't even checked yet to see if they made the finals or not," he said.

"I think they did," I said softly, turning to the list of contestants.

"You're right. They're listed here—April and Candy Stein. And look at this! Wow, one of the pairs of twins they'll be competing against has almost the same name as you do. Her name is Anna Trent. Isn't that wild?"

"Uh, yeah. It sure is," I said.

"Hey, let's try to find out who she is," Bobby suggested eagerly.

"No!" I shouted. "It might be embarrassing."

"Jo, I don't think I've ever seen you embarrassed about anything," he joked.

"Uh, well..." I turned my back and pretended to stare at someone across the room. "Uh, I have to go check on something, Bobby. See you later."

"Wait, Jo. What's wrong?" he called after me, but I was already running away. I knew that I wasn't very good at telling lies, and I didn't want to have to tell any more now.

After searching for a few minutes, I found Joanna sitting at a small table in a dark corner of the room.

"Oh, there you are," she said, standing up and walking over to me. "I was hoping you would walk by here."

"Guess who I've been talking to? Bobby," I said without waiting for her response. "I had to pretend to be you for a while."

"He didn't guess anything, did he?" Joanna asked with wide eyes.

I shook my head. "No. I must be pretty good at being you."

Joanna smiled. "Well, it's time for dinner."

"Already?" I exclaimed.

"Yeah. It's too bad that we can't eat together," Joanna said and winked. "We'd be like real twins."

"Yeah, but we're the next best thing. And we can talk tomorrow before the *big* event," I said dramatically.

"Are you nervous about the contest tomorrow?" Joanna asked.

"Yes. My stomach hurts whenever I think about it," I admitted. But I also knew that seeing the looks on my sisters' faces was going to make it all worthwhile.

"Everything will be fine," Joanna assured me. Well, I guess I'd better go sit with my family, too."

"Okay, see you later," I said as I walked away.

It only took me five minutes to find my family. They were sitting at a table near the front of the huge banquet room. My mom was the first to see me. She pointed to the empty chair next to her like it was a big deal if I sat there.

"Did you have a nice visit with your friend?" Mom asked as I sat down.

"Sure. Joanna is a lot of fun. But I wish she lived near us," I said, glancing across the table to see if my sisters were listening. They weren't. They were busy whispering and giggling about something.

"Where does your friend live?" Dad asked.

"Sacramento," I said.

"That's not far from us," Dad said, reaching for a roll. "I can drive you there sometime for a visit."

"Really? That would be great, Dad! You'll really like Joanna," I told him. "She seems a lot like me."

"Who is Joanna?" Candy interrupted. "Is she a twin?"

I tried to hide a grin. "No, not really," I said mysteriously. Then I stood up quickly so I didn't have to explain what I meant by that comment. "I think I'll go get some food. I'm really hungry."

I couldn't believe how long the buffet line was. After a few minutes of standing, my eyes naturally drifted over to the dessert table. Right in the center of the table was a huge bowl of chocolate mousse, my favorite dessert in the whole world.

I ate my roast beef dinner in record time

and headed for the dessert bar. I grabbed two servings of the mousse and quickly scanned the room for Joanna and her family. After looking the room over twice, I started back toward our table.

Luckily, I glanced in my family's direction before they saw me. I couldn't believe my eyes. Someone was sitting in my chair—and she looked just like me.

What did Joanna think she was doing? I couldn't believe it. Was Joanna telling my family about our plan or was she just pretending to be me?

I moved a little closer to hear what Joanna was saying. I hid behind a pole to stay out of sight.

My dad was saying, "I'd like to relax a little. Let's call it a night. Okay, girls?"

"Okay," April replied.

"Sure," Candy said. "It would feel good to talk a walk. I think I ate too much. What about you, Frankie?"

"Yeah, dinner was great. I'm stuffed, too," Joanna answered.

"What happened to your usual chocolate attack?" April asked.

Joanna fidgeted. "I'm just not as hungry tonight. There's so much to think about. And it's exciting that my sisters made the finals."

"It *is* wonderful," Candy said, looking at Joanna strangely. "We're a cinch to win."

"Really?" Joanna added with a sigh. "It might not be as easy as you think."

Don't give us away, I yelled at Joanna silently. I was getting worried. Sometimes, Joanna liked to live too dangerously. I guess I still had a lot to learn about my new twin.

"What are you talking about, Frankie? Of course, they'll win," my mom said.

"Oh, I don't know," Joanna said. "There are other twins competing against you, and I'd say it's going to be a tough choice for the judges."

"What do you mean, Frankie?" April demanded. "Do you know the other finalists?"

"Two of them...the Trent twins," Joanna said sweetly. "They look really identical. I'd be a little worried if I were you."

"Why?" April asked. Her voice was a little shaky.

"Because everybody has been talking about them. Haven't you heard of them before?" Joanna asked.

"No, I haven't," April replied.

"I haven't, either," Candy added uneasily.

"Don't worry, girls," Dad assured them. "Even if you don't win, you did make it to the finals. That's a high honor in itself."

"But we *will* win," Candy said defensively. "Our red outfits are gorgeous."

April pouted, "Candy, I told you that I don't want to wear the red outfits. They're too bright."

"Well, I love them, so we're going to wear them," Candy demanded.

"No, we aren't," April insisted. "I want to

wear the black and white dresses. They're definitely more stylish."

"No way! We are wearing the red outfits. Don't be such a baby, April."

"A baby?" April yelled. "Stop bossing me around. You always expect me to do what you want me to do, and I'm tired of it."

"Girls, stop fighting," my father said wearily. "You're just tired. You'll both feel better in the morning."

"But, Dad!" April wailed. "Candy's always telling me what to do. It isn't fair."

"Come on, girls. Let's go back to the inn," Mom said.

I watched all of them gather up their stuff and head out of the building. Joanna turned around and saw me watching her. She smiled. I mouthed the words, "What are you doing?"

My dad and the twins had started walking toward the doorway. April and Candy were avoiding each other. Their fights were so stupid. They always ignored each other for a while, and then they made up.

Joanna pointed at my sisters and winked. Then she waved at me and hurried to catch up with my family.

Oh, no! I panicked. She's going home with my family. *What am I going to do now?*

It seemed like I only had one choice. I had to find Joanna's brothers and let them think I was Joanna. I had absolutely no idea how I was going to pull it off.

Things are getting too crazy for me, I decided. *I'm not so sure I like being a twin after all.*

Seven

"THERE you are, Joanna," a woman's voice called from behind me.

I turned around and looked up into Mrs. Trent's blue eyes. She seemed annoyed.

"Joanna," she said impatiently, "I've been looking all over for you. We're all ready to go up to our rooms now. There's not much point in staying around here."

I took a deep breath. Somehow I had to get through this evening without Joanna's family finding out our secret.

"Are you ready to leave?" Mrs. Trent asked.

"I guess so," I said. Mrs. Trent always seemed to be in a rush.

"Well, let's go," she said.

What choice do I have? I thought. I shrugged helplessly and followed Mrs. Trent out of the banquet room.

Joanna had told me that she was sharing a suite with her parents and that her brothers had a room across the hall.

I decided that pretending to be Joanna wouldn't be so bad, especially if it was just for one night. Joanna couldn't be that different from me, could she? I found her suitcase and picked out a flannel nightgown.

But before I could change, there was a knock at my door. I looked up to see one of Joanna's brothers open the door a crack.

"Joanna, do you have a minute?" he asked. "I want to ask you about something."

"About what?" I asked, putting the nightgown down.

"About girls. I mean, I already told you I kind of like April Stein."

I was relieved that this was Bobby I was talking to. I thought he seemed really nice.

"I don't really know how I can help," I said.

"Just listen, okay?" Bobby asked me. He seemed a little nervous.

"Sure, Bobby."

"I talked to April tonight, and I can't believe how great she is. But the problem is that I want her to like me, too," he admitted, sitting down next to me on the bed. "You'll help me, won't you?"

I felt panicky inside. "What can I do?"

"I was telling April about the flips that you showed me how to do last week. She seemed really impressed that I could do something unusual and asked me to show them to her. But I chickened out, because I'd only tried them once. Could you show me how to do them again?" Bobby asked.

"I don't know anything about gym—" I barely stopped myself from letting Bobby know that I wasn't Joanna. I had almost admitted to knowing absolutely nothing about gymnastics. That would have given away our secret for sure. How was I going to get out of this one?

Bobby looked worried. "Please help me, Jo. It'll just take a few minutes. April's a neat girl, and I want her to like me."

"I'd like to help, Bobby, but I can't do flips in a hotel room. And it's too late to go down to the beach," I said, quickly. "Maybe we could work on it tomorrow."

"I'm meeting April in the morning. I wanted to think up something special that I could do to impress her," he explained. "I want her to know that I like her."

"Hey, I've got it," I said.

"What?"

I smiled. "I'll help you write a poem for her. It'll be just the kind of thing to impress her."

Bobby looked stunned. "Poetry? I don't know, Jo. Since when have you been able to write? English has never been your best subject."

"Just give me a sheet of paper and a pencil.

Then we'll see who isn't good at English. You're about to see a new side of your sister," I said with a grin.

Two hours later, I crawled into Joanna's bed. I was exhausted, but happy to have helped Bobby. The poem was short but terrific. I knew that April would be thrilled when Bobby gave it to her. And for a little while, it seemed like Bobby really was my brother.

The door slowly opened, and Joanna's mother walked in. She was staring at me strangely.

"You're going to bed without an argument?" she asked.

"It's been a long day. I'm beat," I explained.

"I guess it has been a long day," she said. Then she smiled, which softened her face and made her look nicer than she looked at the banquet. "I can't believe you're not going to beg me to let you stay up and watch TV. What did you do today, Joanna? Anything that was interesting?"

I tried not to giggle. Yes, a lot of interesting things had happened that day. But I couldn't tell Mrs. Trent that the real Joanna was a few miles away with my family, and that I was just sitting there pretending to be her daughter.

"Yeah, I made a friend," I told her finally.

I laid back against the pillow and yawned.

Joanna's mother bent over and kissed me lightly on the cheek.

"Pleasant dreams, Joanna."

"Thanks. Good-night, Mom."

I thought I'd fall into a deep sleep the second Mrs. Trent closed the door behind her. But instead I tossed and turned for hours. When I did sleep, I had horrible nightmares that Joanna's family, my family, and total strangers were pointing at me and screaming, "You can't fool us! You're not a real twin."

* * * * *

I sat up in bed to shut out the screaming voices in my head. I saw that the sun was shining through the window. Then I remembered. Today was the Lookalike Contest finals, and I was Joanna.

I could hear the phone ringing in the next room.

Mr. Trent called, "Joanna, there's a phone call for you."

I jumped out of bed and ran into the next room.

Mr. Trent was holding the phone out to me. "It's a girl named Frankie."

"I met her at the beach," I explained as I took the phone from him. Boy, was I mad at her for getting me into this crazy mess. "Frankie," I said into the phone. "I'm glad you called."

Mr. Trent walked into the bathroom where Mrs. Trent was brushing her hair in front of a huge mirror.

"Jo, why did you do this?" I asked her.

"I wanted to see if I could fool your family," Joanna said. "And it worked. Candy and April kept me talking till way past midnight."

"They *what*?" I nearly shouted. I was shocked. Candy and April never included me in any girl talk. What was going on?

"Yeah, we talked for hours. It was great. You're really lucky to have such neat sisters."

"Neat sisters? Are you crazy?" I asked her.

"I really like your sisters. I'd trade them for my brothers any day."

I thought about writing the poem with Bobby the night before. I'd rather be related to him than to my sisters any day. "Well, I happen to think your brothers are great, especially Bobby. They're better than my stuck-up..." I stopped myself from saying sisters just as Joanna's parents walked into the room.

"They are not stuck up," Joanna said. "They were great, but they were wondering why I was being nice to them."

"They're the ones who aren't nice to me!" I said. Joanna's mother gave me a strange look, so I lowered my voice. "You've got it wrong."

"I think *you* do, but we don't have time to argue about it. We have to meet somewhere and switch back."

I looked at the pink watch on my wrist. "How about in an hour at the boardwalk bandstand? That way, we can check out what it's going to be like later during the, uh, big event."

"Okay. Be sure to wear the blue T-shirt, okay?"

I smiled. "Where is it?"

"It's in my suitcase. I already have yours on. Your sisters can't figure out what the words on the T-shirt mean, and it's driving them crazy," Joanna said.

I laughed. "I can imagine. The words don't make any sense unless they're read with both shirts together. But they'll find out soon enough what they mean."

"Your sisters are coming back. I have to

go," Joanna said.

"But—" I said as the line clicked dead. I had to get moving if I wanted to be Frankie again.

Eight

"WHAT happened to you?" I asked Joanna as she plopped down beside me on one of the bandstand's folding chairs. She was nearly half an hour late.

Joanna tossed her reddish hair to one side and grinned. "Sorry, but I had trouble fitting into your shoes. I had no idea you had such big feet."

"My feet are not big!" I defended myself.

"Compared to mine, they are," Joanna said.

I looked down at Joanna's feet. She was wearing my new shoes—the ones I had been saving for a special occasion. The shoes looked great on me, but they looked ridiculous on Joanna's feet.

"Why didn't you just wear your sandals again like I did?" I asked her.

"Because my yellow sandals would have looked stupid with my blue shirt. These shoes are much better, even if they are too big. And it also wasn't easy to get away from your sisters."

"My sisters?" I asked. "Why were they a problem? They don't know about us, do they?"

"No way!" Joanna insisted. "I wouldn't tell them."

"I hope not. I just don't understand why they would talk to you. I mean, they never talk to me. What did you do to them?"

Joanna shrugged. "Nothing. I just mentioned that I had talked to the Trips, and that I knew a lot about them from their sister. Your sisters asked me a million questions about Brandon and Bobby. But I had to be careful about how much I told them."

Now I understood why my sisters would be so interested in talking with Joanna. I didn't feel quite so jealous then.

Joanna was looking at my T-shirt that said "I'm Her." It was really her T-shirt, but I was wearing it for now.

"Want to switch shirts so we're wearing our own?" I asked.

"Yeah. Let's go find a rest room along the boardwalk," Joanna suggested.

As we walked along the boardwalk, I noticed that people were staring at us. They were the same kind of stares that my sisters got whenever they went places together. I had always envied the attention they got. Now, it was my turn to have some fun. For now, I could overlook the trick that Joanna had pulled on me last night.

After we had switched into our own shirts, we set out to have some fun before the Lookalike Contest began in less than two hours.

Joanna suddenly pointed to nine strange mirrors. "Come on," she urged. "They're funhouse mirrors. Let's see our double images!"

We stepped in front of the first mirror and giggled at our gawky, long legs. The second mirror chopped off our heads and gave us a total of eight legs. By the time we had posed before all nine mirrors, we were giggling uncontrollably.

"We still have some time before the contest," I said. "Let's check out the arcade games."

"Sure. But we'd better keep an eye out for our families. We don't want to blow everything now," Joanna said seriously.

"We really need to stay away from Bobby," I added with a giggle. "He's probably pretty suspicious of me—I mean you."

"What are you talking about?" Joanna asked.

"You wrote a poem for him to give to April," I explained. "He wanted to do something that would impress her, even though I can't imagine why."

"I've never written a poem in my life. I hate anything that has to do with writing," she said.

"That was the old Joanna," I told her. "The new Joanna wrote a poem last night."

"Frankie! You didn't!"

"It was either that or attempt a back flip. And there was no way that I could do that. I didn't want to break my neck," I said.

"But Bobby must have guessed that you weren't me! He's really smart," Joanna wailed.

"I had no choice. And it serves you right anyway. You shouldn't have pretended to be me. It wasn't fun being stranded, you know. You're just lucky that I'm so nice," I added. "Besides, our secret will be out in the open soon anyway."

"I guess making you stay with my family last night was a little bit mean," Joanna admitted. "But I thought it was fun. I really like your sisters. I don't think you've given them a chance."

"I could say the same about your brothers," I added.

"Maybe," she replied with a shrug. "I also

don't agree that your sisters would tell the judges about us—if they knew, I mean."

"Yes, they would. Believe me," I replied defensively.

"No, they wouldn't. I think deep down that they really care about you. And they wouldn't hurt you like that," Joanna said.

"You're wrong. And the more I think about it, the more nervous I'm getting about standing up on that bandstand," I admitted. "April and Candy will be right there, too. And I'm scared of what they're going to do."

"What are you talking about?" Joanna asked.

"Once April and Candy realize there are two of us, they'll announce to everybody that we aren't really twins. It will be totally embarrassing," I said.

"You don't want to quit now, do you?" Joanna asked, looking worried.

I shook my head. "No, I'm not a quitter."

Joanna sighed and glanced down at her

silver watch. "There's something that I want to do before the contest. Will you wait here for me? It will only take a minute."

"What are you going to do?" I asked.

"Well," Joanna paused, "I'll tell you if you promise you won't get mad."

"Of course, I won't get mad. What is it?"

Joanna hesitated. She took a deep breath and blurted, "I want to wish your sisters good luck."

Nine

"YOU want to do what?" I shrieked. "We'll be standing next to my sisters on the bandstand in just a little while. Don't mess things up now by saying something that you shouldn't or by making them suspicious."

"I won't," Joanna said calmly. "I just really want to call them to wish them good luck. They were really nice to me. They're the big sisters I've always wanted."

"But, Joanna," I began, realizing it was no use. I watched her walk off toward the pay phones. Joanna definitely was stubborn. That was for sure.

I walked down the stairs that led from the boardwalk to the beach. I took my shoes off and played tag with the waves rolling into shore. Just as I was wondering if things could get any worse, I heard someone yell "Joanna" in my direction. I turned to see all three of the triplets looking at me.

"Hi, Jo," one of them said.

"What's with the T-shirt?" another Trip asked.

"It's just a shirt," I said quickly, folding my hands over my chest to hide the words "She's Me."

"But what do the words mean?" the last Trip insisted.

"Yeah, what does it mean, Joanna? You seem different lately somehow," the first one said. He grinned, and I knew it was Bobby.

I faked a laugh. "What are you talking about?"

"Oh, there are quite a few things that seem weird," the same Trip replied. "Like, why did you nearly freak out on the Jet Star? And why did you panic when I asked you to do a flip?

And the poetry? You've never liked to write. What's going on?" Bobby stared at me and waited for an answer.

"Joanna wrote a poem?" one of the brothers asked. "I don't believe it."

I met Bobby's gaze. Then, suddenly, he winked at me. He had guessed! He knew I wasn't his sister! And I had been worried about Joanna telling my sisters the truth. Instead, I had blown our cover.

"So, what's going on?" the second Trip repeated.

Bobby turned to his brother and said, "Oh, I guess Joanna is going through a phase where she wants to try out new personalities. She's always been unpredictable. Now, she's just being weird, too."

"But how could Jo write a poem?" the Trip demanded.

Bobby laughed. "I admit it was pretty good for Joanna. It wasn't an English classic or anything, but April loved it. Hey, I still have a few ride tickets left if you want to do a few before the contest begins. But I want to be there in time to see April and Candy on the bandstand."

"Me, too," Brandon agreed. "Candy said she was a little nervous. I want to be there to cheer her on."

"So, let's get going then," Steve added.

"See you later, Jo," Bobby said with a grin. "Like maybe at the Lookalike Contest?"

I nodded and giggled. Bobby was great! I wished he really was my brother.

Suddenly, I felt those butterflies again. "Yeah, I'll be there. I wouldn't miss it for the world."

* * * * *

The Lookalike Contest was underway. The boys' competition would be first, followed by the mixed category and the girls' event. Joanna and I bumped into each other in the rest room.

We gave each other a quick hug before going out to sign in officially for the competition.

"Are you still nervous?" Joanna asked me.

"Yeah. But I won't chicken out," I assured her.

"Well, it's too late now. Hey, look," Joanna said as she pointed to the stage. "There are the winners of the boys' contest."

I looked to the center of the stage, where two tiny boys were jumping up and down and screaming. *It would be more exciting if Joanna's brothers had won,* I decided.

I stopped talking during the mixed-category competition. It was fun to watch brothers and sisters who looked so much alike.

"I think the second ones should win," I whispered to Joanna.

"No way. I think the fifth couple should win," Joanna said.

The trophy went to couple number five a few minutes later.

"How did you know?" I asked Joanna.

"It was just a lucky guess," she replied with a grin. "Uh-oh. It's almost time." Even Joanna looked a little worried. "Do you really think your sisters will blow our cover?"

"Yeah, I do. But they'll be too surprised at first to do anything, and by then we'll be up on the bandstand," I said. "It won't help to worry now. We'll just do our best and hope that we win."

"At least we have the rules on our side," Joanna reminded me. "There's nothing written in the rules that specifies we have to be sisters."

I nodded. "Yeah."

Then we heard "Candy and April Stein" announced over the loudspeaker.

"Oh, there they go toward the stage," I said. My stomach began to act up by doing its flip-flop routine.

"Wow! Candy and April look really pretty," Joanna gushed.

The judge asked April and Candy some simple questions, like where they lived and what they would like to be when they get older. I was amazed to realize that I was very proud of my sisters. They were so confident and determined. But I never would have told them that.

I was even more surprised at April's answer when one of the judges asked her why she wanted to win the contest. "I want our family to be proud of us," she said. Was this my sister saying all this mushy stuff?

"They really mean it," Joanna whispered into my ear. "I told you they weren't so bad."

"I hope you're right," I said. Our moment of truth was coming up.

The crowd applauded as my sisters left the stage. And then it happened. Our names were called.

"Anna and Francesca Trent," the announcer called out loudly.

"This is it," Joanna said, stepping forward.

We walked up the stairs and across the stage. I didn't dare let myself look at the audience. I didn't want to see any shocked looks from our families.

The judge asked us simple questions, too. I let Joanna answer most of them. I jumped in to answer the ones that didn't seem like lying, like how old we were and who thought up the idea for our T-shirts.

After a few minutes, I began to relax. I felt better until I looked behind me and saw the shocked looks on April and Candy's faces.

Oh, no, I thought, *here it comes. My sisters are going to tell the whole world that I'm not really a twin.*

I glanced back again and saw that Candy and April were whispering. It was making me incredibly nervous all over again.

Joanna was still talking, but I had stopped listening. I was terrified. I couldn't take my eyes off of my sisters. What were they going to do? Just one word from them would ruin everything for Joanna and me.

Finally, both April and Candy looked over at me. And they were smiling! April even gave me a thumbs-up sign. She wasn't going to give us away. I couldn't believe it!

The world's biggest miracle had just happened. My sisters were on my side!

Ten

THE judges were telling us to step back beside the Stein twins, but my feet wouldn't move. I was in shock. Could Joanna have been right about my sisters all along?

"Are you okay, Frankie?" Joanna whispered after she had pulled me back into the lineup of contestants.

"Yeah. I'm just surprised. That's all. I really thought my sisters would mess things up. But they didn't."

"Of course, they didn't," Joanna said. "I told you that they were okay."

I looked over at my sisters. Both of them were grinning at us. For the first time in my life, I was happy to be standing next to them.

April was standing beside me. "Hey, good luck," I whispered to her.

April's eyes widened, but she didn't have a chance to say anything, because one of the judges stood up to thank all of us for entering the contest. There were five sets of contestants in our category.

"And the winners are..." the judge began finally. He looked down at a sheet of paper in his hand. "The winners are Candy and April Stein! Step forward, girls."

I jumped up with joy. My sisters had won. And the weird thing was that I was glad—really glad.

"I told you they were okay," Joanna said again. "Maybe the problem has been that you think of them as the Princess Twins, instead of just two people."

"Maybe you're right," I said thoughtfully.

Suddenly, my mom and dad were rushing up onto the stage. I thought they were going over to congratulate my sisters, but instead they came over to me and Joanna.

"Frankie!" my mom exclaimed, looking in confusion from Joanna to me.

"Hi, Mom," I said.

"Is it still Frankie, or should I call you Francesca?" Mom asked. I couldn't tell whether she was going to yell at me or laugh.

"I'm still Frankie, Mom. I can explain everything."

"It's unbelievable," Mom went on. Then she smiled. "I honestly didn't know which one of you was my daughter. I want to hear the whole story behind this."

Joanna laughed.

Then Dad said with a grin, "I don't know if I've gained a daughter or lost one."

Joanna and I shared a long look, and then our explanations tumbled out. Somewhere in the middle, Joanna's parents, her brothers, and my sisters crowded around to listen. By the time we were finished, everyone was amazed by our twin adventure. I was just

relieved that everybody was smiling.

I noticed that April was staring strangely at Joanna. "It was you last night, wasn't it?" she finally asked Joanna. "That's why Frankie seemed so different. It wasn't Frankie at all."

"You're right," Joanna admitted. "But I had a great time last night. And I learned a lot, too."

"About what?" Candy asked.

I jumped in before Joanna could answer. "We both found out that having someone who looks just like you isn't always as easy or exciting as it seems to be."

"We could have told you that," April said, nudging Candy.

"I also found out that you guys are pretty cool. I'm glad you won the Lookalike Contest," I said.

"You're glad we won?" Candy asked in surprise.

"Yeah. It was fun just feeling like a twin for a while," I said.

April smiled at Bobby. They said good-bye to us and headed toward the boardwalk. Candy and Brandon left a few minutes later, saying they were going swimming one last time before we all had to leave for home.

"I just can't get over it," Joanna's mom was saying to my mom. "Getting used to triplets was hard enough. Now my daughter has a twin, too!"

"Our daughters are something else," Mr. Trent said, looking amused.

"They certainly are," Joanna's mom agreed. "I guess we can't be angry at them. They must have worked hard to look so much alike. And then to get up on that bandstand..." She shook her head and smiled.

"Well, we're all lucky that Frankie and Joanna don't live in the same house," Dad added. "One set of multiple kids is enough for any family."

I suddenly felt sad. Joanna and I had spent so much time together during the last couple of days. I was really going to miss her. I looked over at her, and she looked upset, too.

Our parents were busy talking, so I pulled Joanna aside. "Hey, let's go down to the boardwalk one last time," I suggested.

"That sounds great," Joanna said.

"You know, it's been an amazing vacation," I admitted as we walked down the beach. "We found out that being a twin or triplet isn't so perfect all the time. But it does have its fun moments..."

Joanna grinned. "Yeah, I guess we really shocked everyone. I know we shouldn't have done it, but it was fun. And I am going to miss having a twin. I like all of the attention," she said.

"Me, too, after I got used to it. But Sacramento and Davis really aren't that far apart," I pointed out.

"Yeah, maybe our families will visit sometime," Joanna said with an excited look in her eyes. "And just think of all the crazy things we can do when we get together..."

"Hey, wait a second," I said. "Let's just work on being friends for a while, okay?"

Joanna gave me one of her impatient looks, but then she smiled. "Yeah, you're right. Being friends is a lot more important than being twins."

"I'm starved," I said as we climbed the steps to the boardwalk. "Let's get something to eat."

Joanna giggled. "Just lead the way, twin, I mean friend."

About the Author

LINDA JOY SINGLETON has had a best friend since she was 10 years old. Linda and Lori have done just about everything together, including starting up a newspaper and a fudge business. When they were younger, they often pretended that they were twins.

Linda has always enjoyed books and remembers writing her first short story at the age of nine. When she was 14, she spent an entire Christmas vacation writing a 200-page mystery about a haunted mirror maze.

Almost Twins is Linda's first published book. Besides writing, Linda enjoys long walks, bicycling, and square dancing.

Linda lives on a three-acre ranch near Sacramento, California. She and her husband, David, have a daughter, a son, and a whole barnyard of animals, including horses, goats, chickens, and ducks. They also have seven cats and dogs.